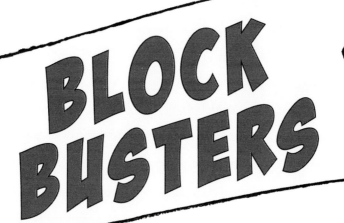

Librarian Reviewer
Chris Kreie
Media Specialist, Eden Prairie Schools, MN
MS in Information Media, St. Cloud State University, MN

Reading Consultant
Mary Evenson
Middle School Teacher, Edina Public Schools, MN
MA in Education, University of Minnesota

First published in the United States in 2008
by Stone Arch Books
151 Good Counsel Drive, P.O. Box 669
Mankato, Minnesota 56002
www.stonearchbooks.com

First published by Evans Brothers Ltd
2A Portman Mansions, Chiltern Street
London W1U 6NR, United Kingdom

Library of Congress Cataloging-in-Publication Data
Lawrie, Robin.
    Block Busters / by Robin and Chris Lawrie; illustrated by Robin
Lawrie.
        p. cm. — (Ridge Riders)
        Summary: The members of the Ridge Riders mountain biking
team use sports psychology to conquer their individual fears of riding
in the cross-country race.
        ISBN 978-1-4342-0484-4 (library binding)
        ISBN 978-1-4342-0544-5 (paperback)
        [1. All terrain cycling—Fiction. 2. Bicycle racing—Fiction. 3. Fear—
Fiction. 4. Cartoons and comics.] I. Lawrie, Christine. II. Title. III. Title:
Blockbusters.
PZ7.L438218Bl 2008
[Fic]—dc22   2007029139

1 2 3 4 5 6 13 12 11 10 09 08

Printed in the United States of America

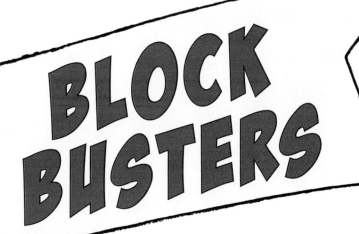

BLOCK BUSTERS

by Robin and Chris Lawrie
illustrated by Robin Lawrie

STONE ARCH BOOKS
MINNEAPOLIS   SAN DIEGO

The Ridge Riders

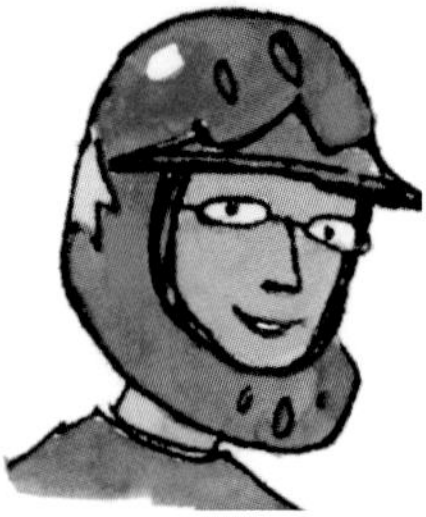

Hi, my name is "Slam" Duncan.

This is Aziz. 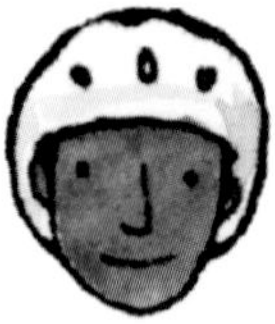 We call him Dozy.

Then there's Larry. 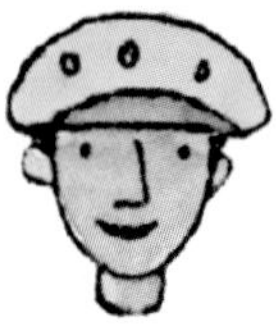

This is Fiona. 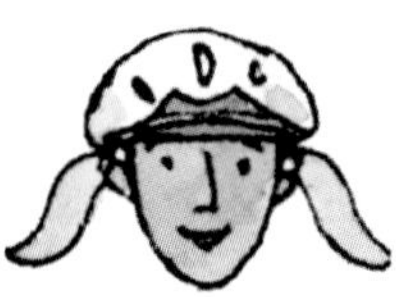

And Andy. 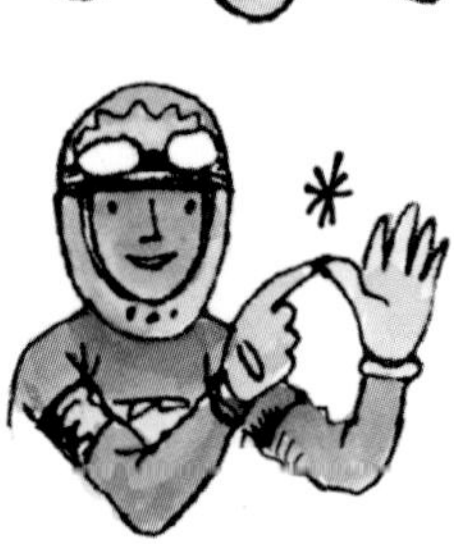
*

* *I'm Andy. (Andy is deaf. He uses sign language instead of talking.)*

 Lately we've been competing in a race series called the Sword in the Stump Challenge.

The challenge is for cross-country riders and downhillers, too.

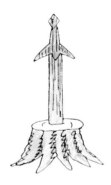

The idea is to promote sportsmanship and fair play by making us think about King Arthur and the Knights of the Round Table.

King Arthur had to pull a sword out of a stone, remember?

We are halfway through the series. The next race is the second cross-country event.

We all had big problems in the first cross-country race. We hadn't scored any points, so we were nervous about the second one. Last year, Larry had broken his leg on a steep drop on the course. So this time, he got scared when he got to the drop in the last race.

Now, he couldn't do it at all.

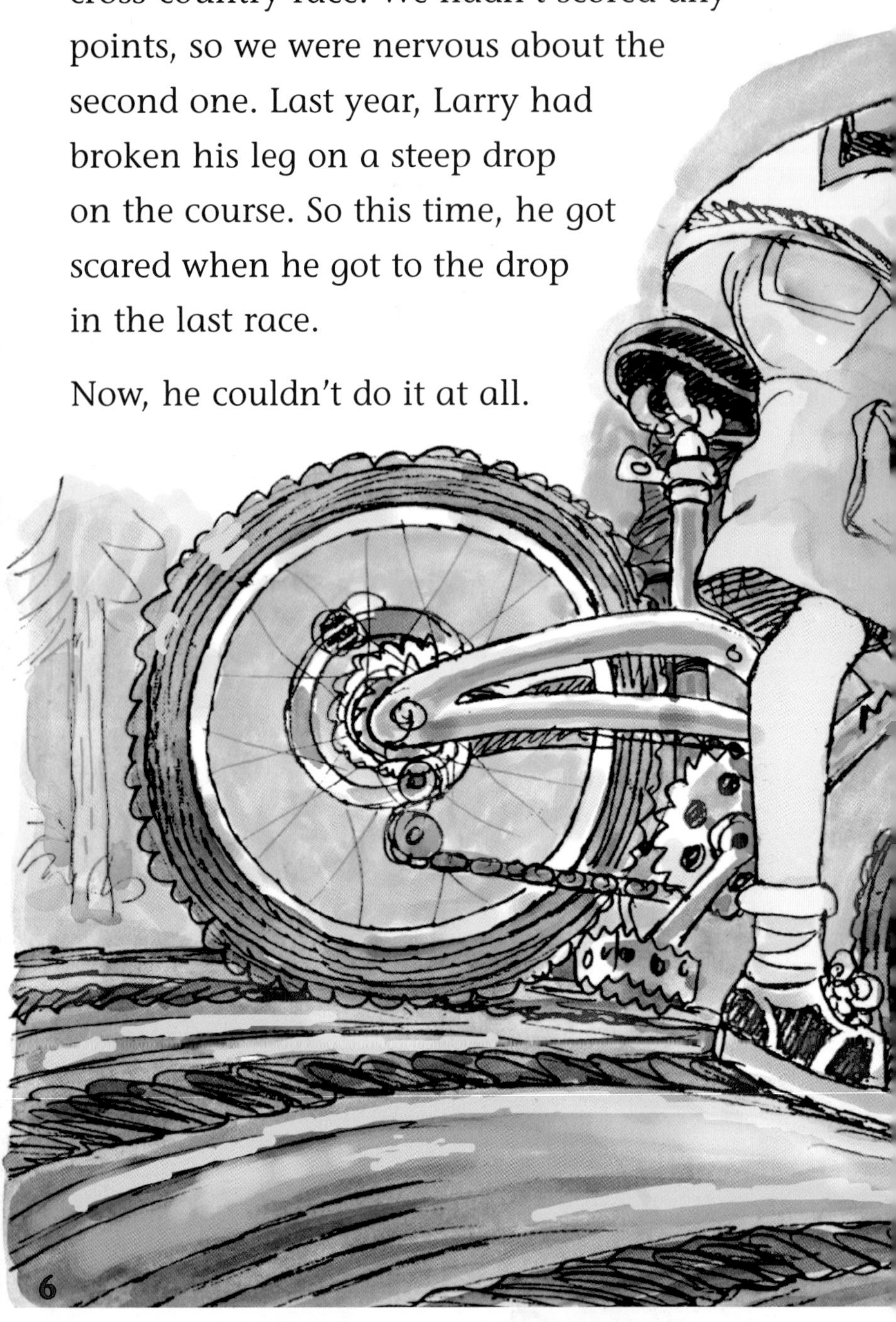

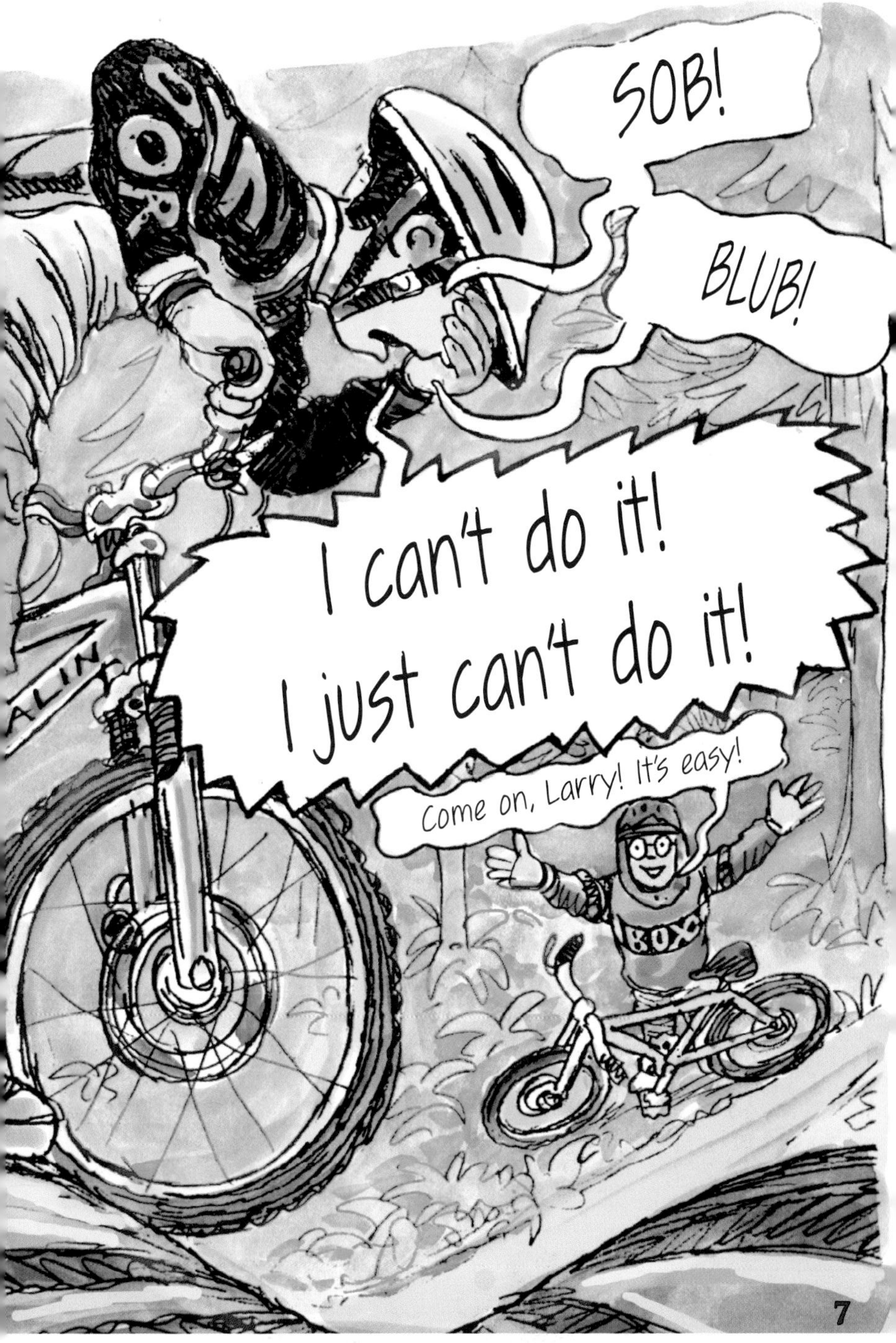
SOB!
BLUB!
I can't do it!
I just can't do it!
Come on, Larry! It's easy!
BOX
ALIN

Some spectators had been rude to Fiona in the last race. It made her lose her confidence.

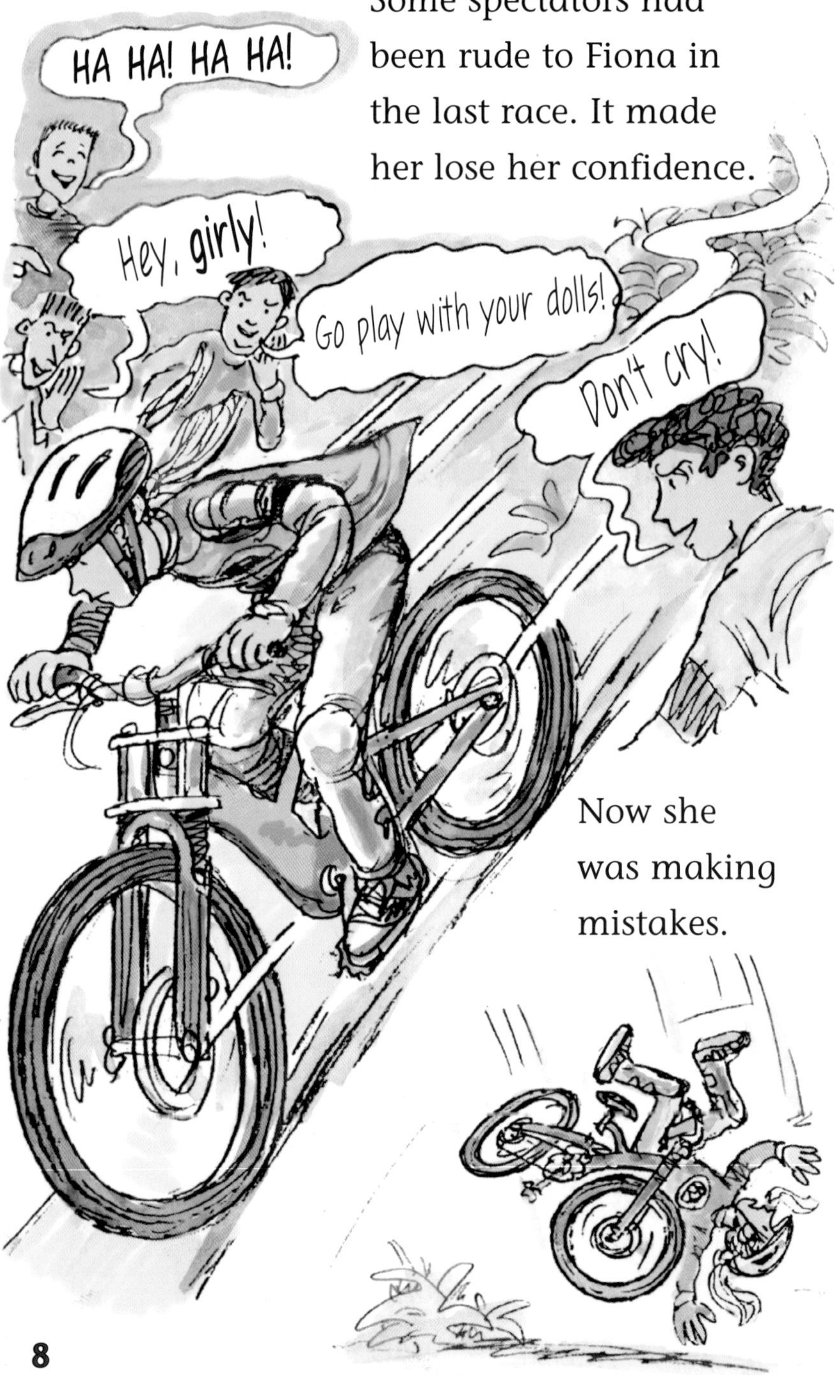
HA HA! HA HA!
Hey, girly!
Go play with your dolls!
Don't cry!

Now she was making mistakes.

Dozy had been using the wrong tires. He really messed up his bike. He was determined not to make the same mistake again.

So he looked up information about tires and saved it on his computer.

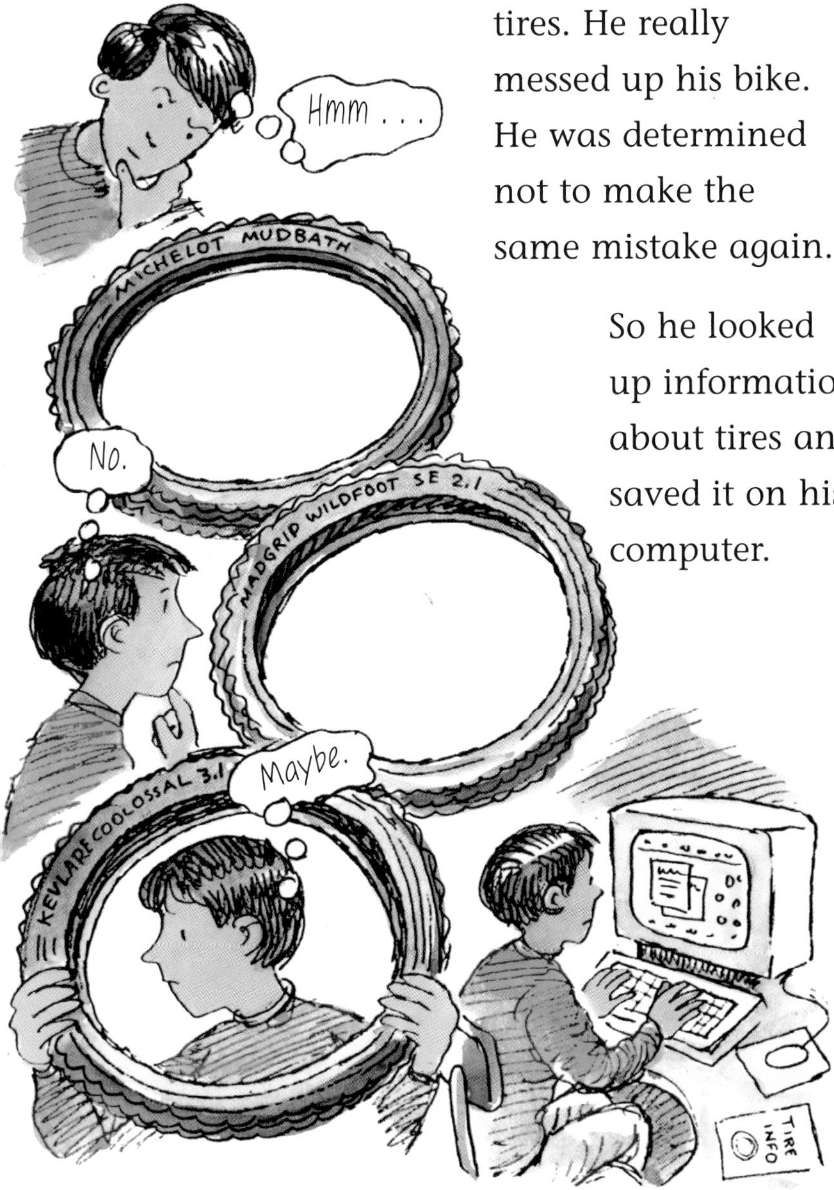
Hmm . . .
MICHELOT MUDBATH
No.
MADGRIP WILDFOOT SE 2.1
KEVLARE COOLOSSAL 3.1
Maybe.
TIRE INFO

Andy had a different problem. He had a bad crash during the last cross-country race. He had been unable to hear a rider trying to get past him. So the rider had pushed him off the track. Andy was afraid it would happen again.

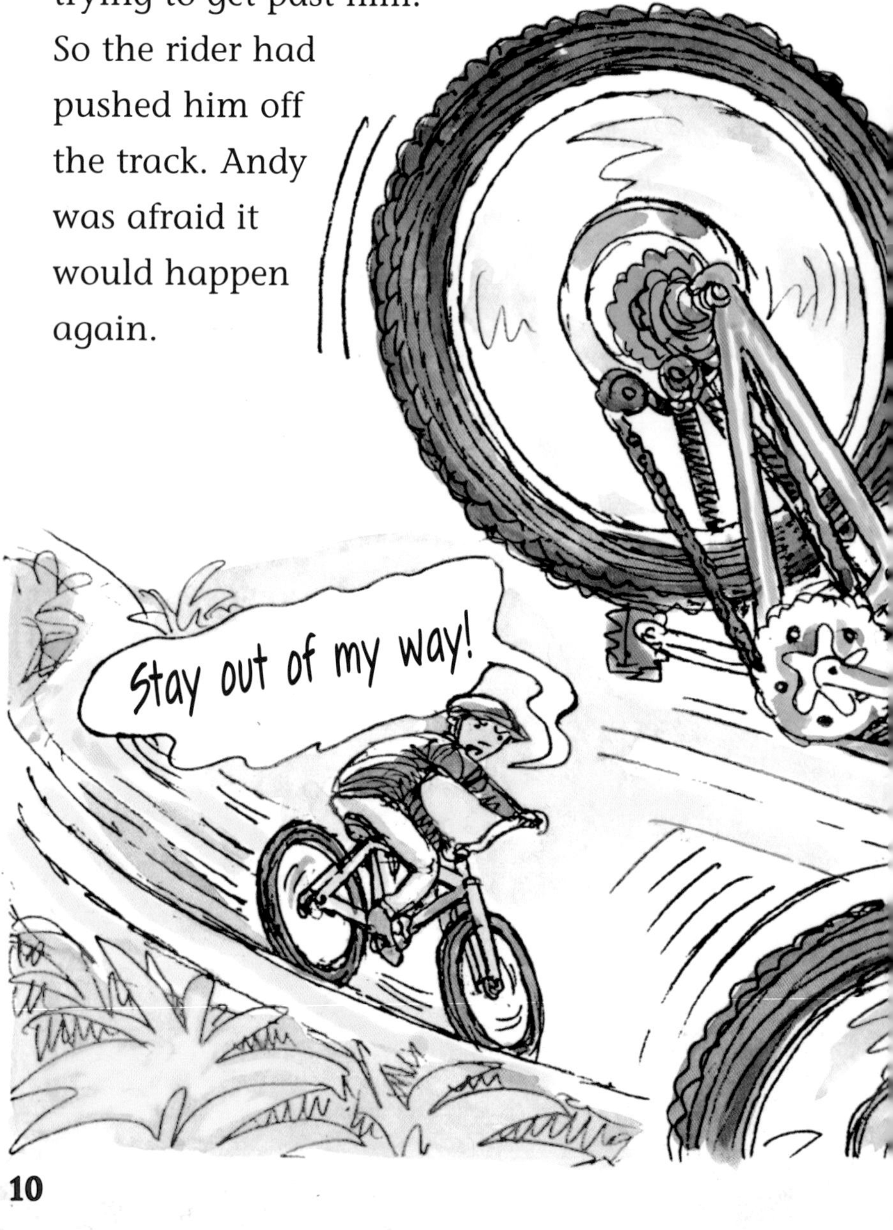
Stay out of my way!

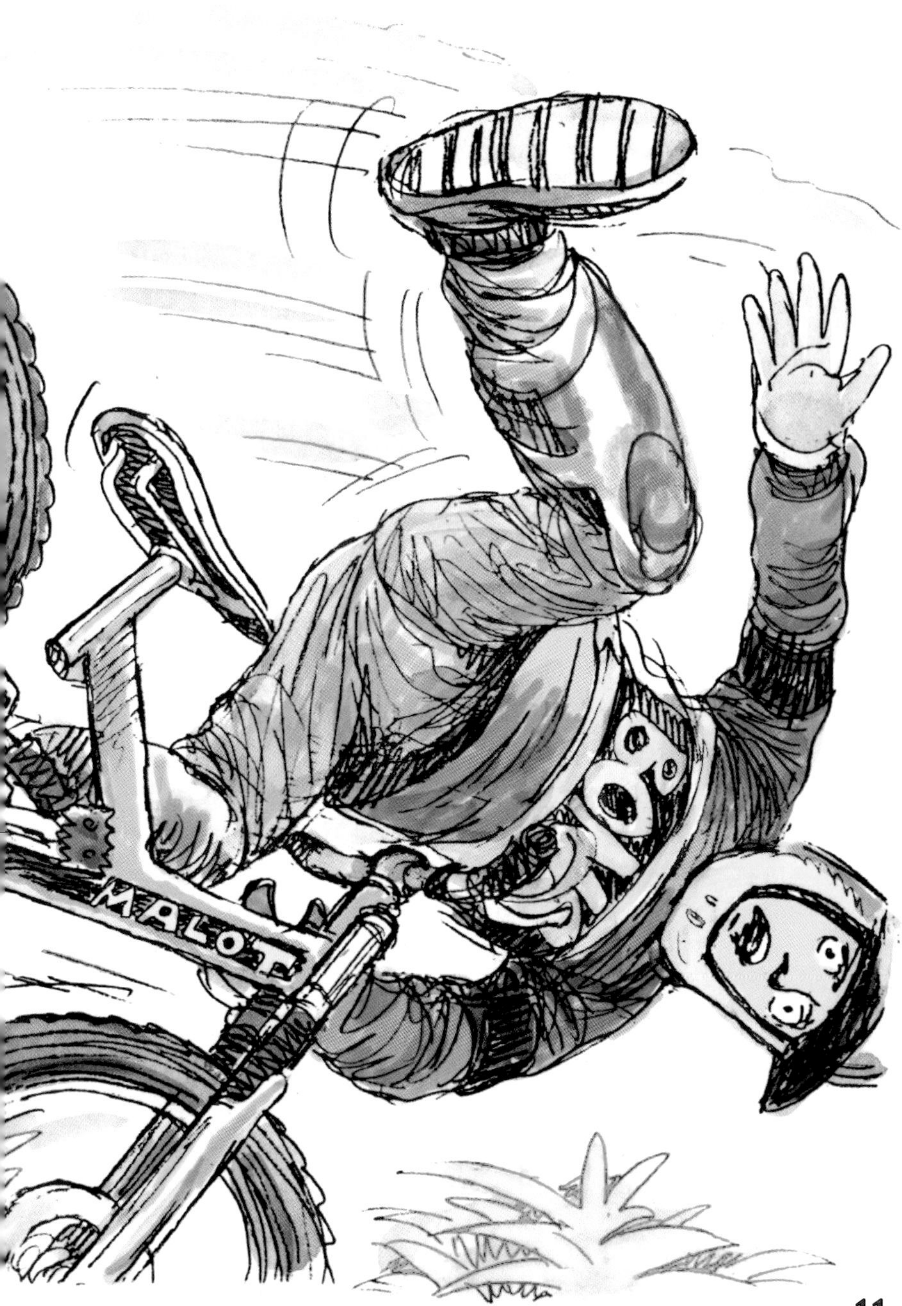
MALOT

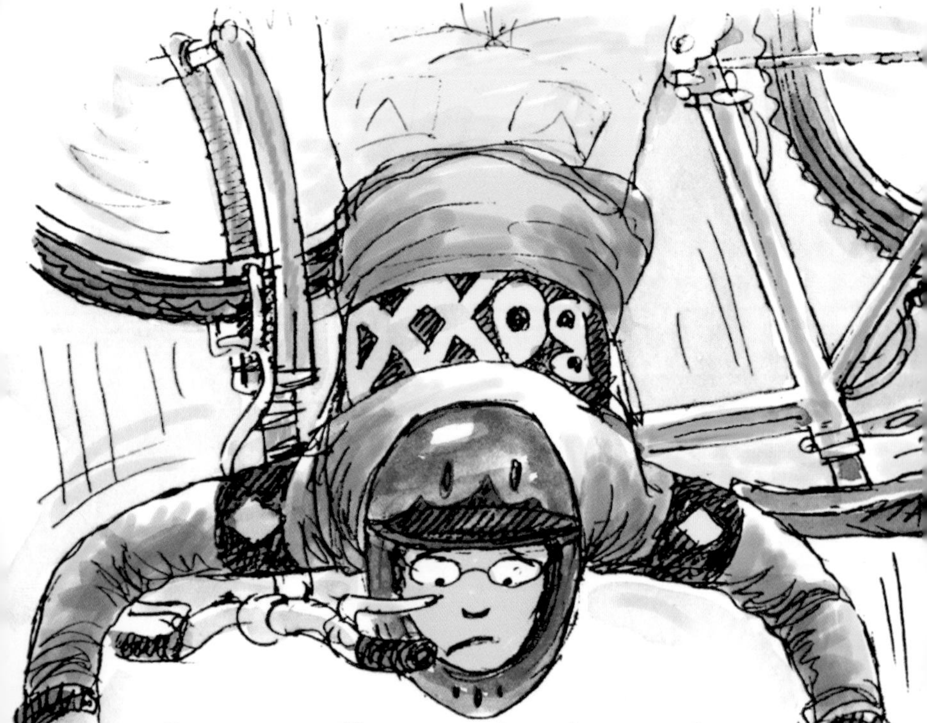

I never really got going during the last race. I was crashing a lot. I thought it was because my reactions were getting slow.

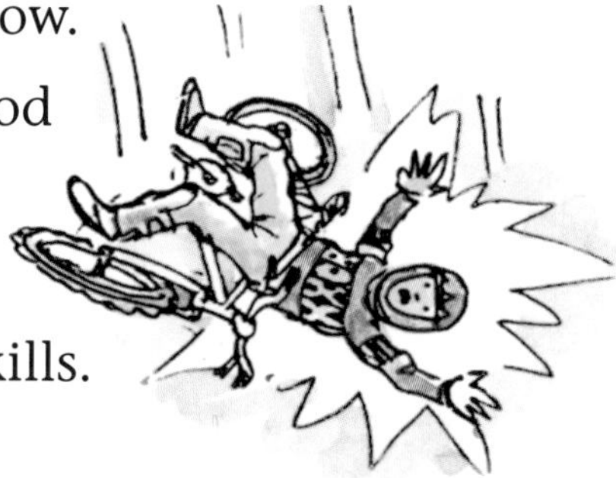

I decided a good computer game could sharpen my skills.

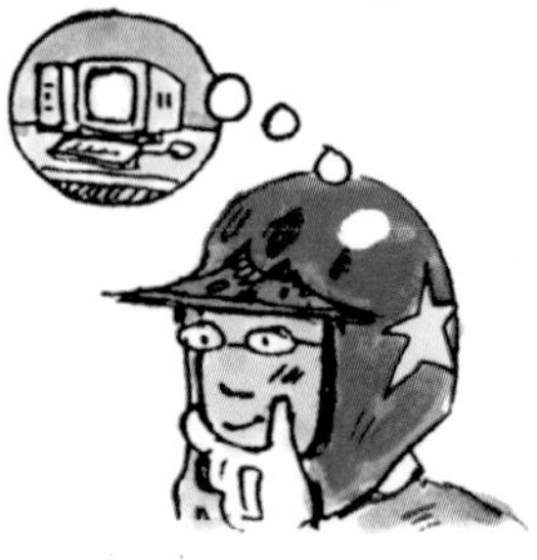

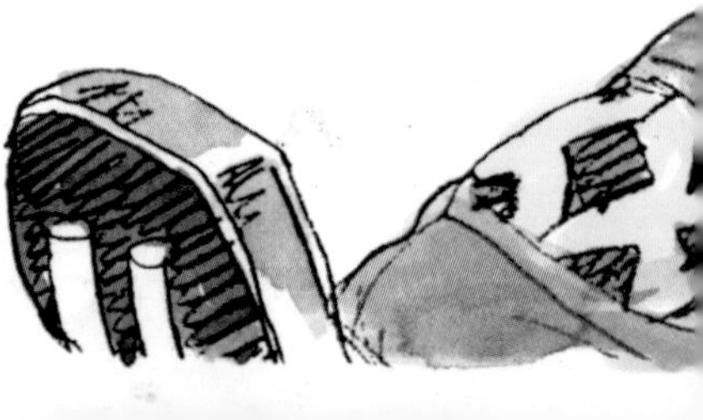

So I scraped the mud off my bike and paid a visit to Steady Eddy's booth in the flea market.

I bought "Space Bikers." It was very cheap and looked like fun.

I couldn't wait to play it, but when I tried to install it . . .

PING!

SORRY. OUT OF MEMORY

EDDY'S GAMES

FILE EDIT VIEW SPECIAL HELP

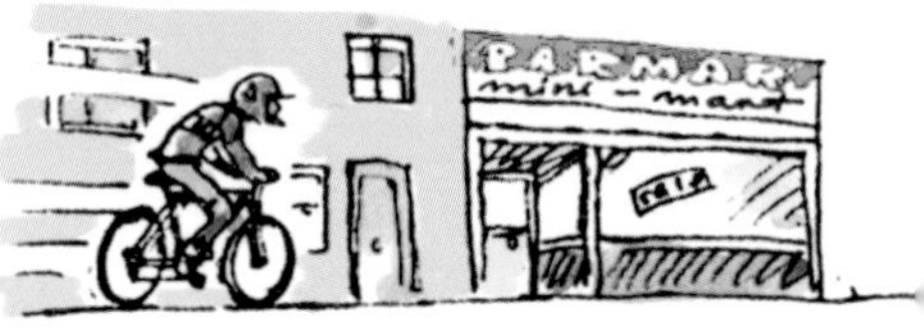
PARMAR
mini — mart

I knew that Dozy's computer had a lot of memory, so I went over to his house. He wasn't home, but his mom said I could wait for him in his room.

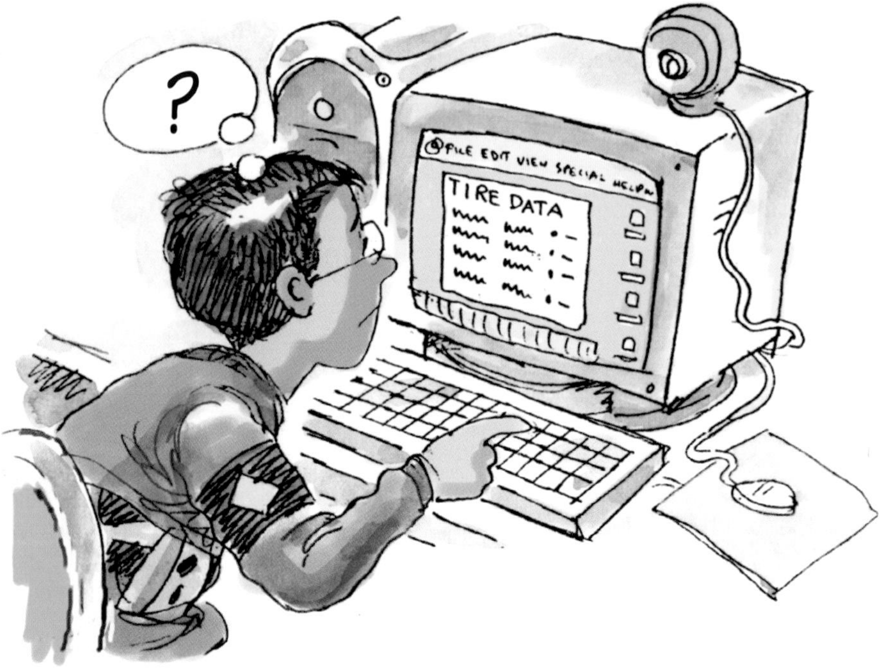
?
FILE EDIT VIEW SPECIAL HELP
TIRE DATA

His computer was on. There was a lot of stuff about tires on it. It looked boring, so I pressed some buttons and made it all disappear.

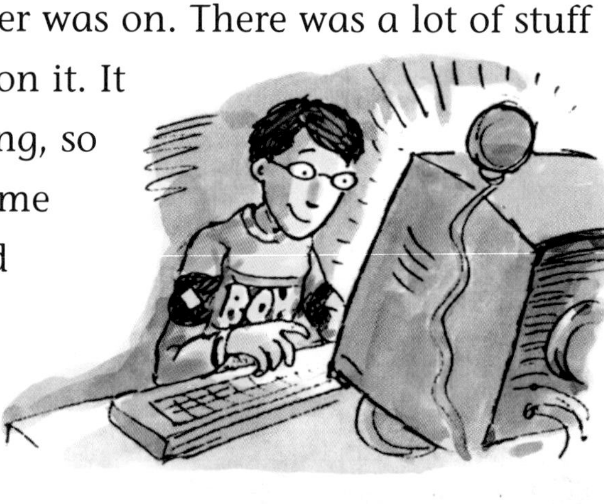

I loaded "Space Bikers" and waited a few minutes . . .

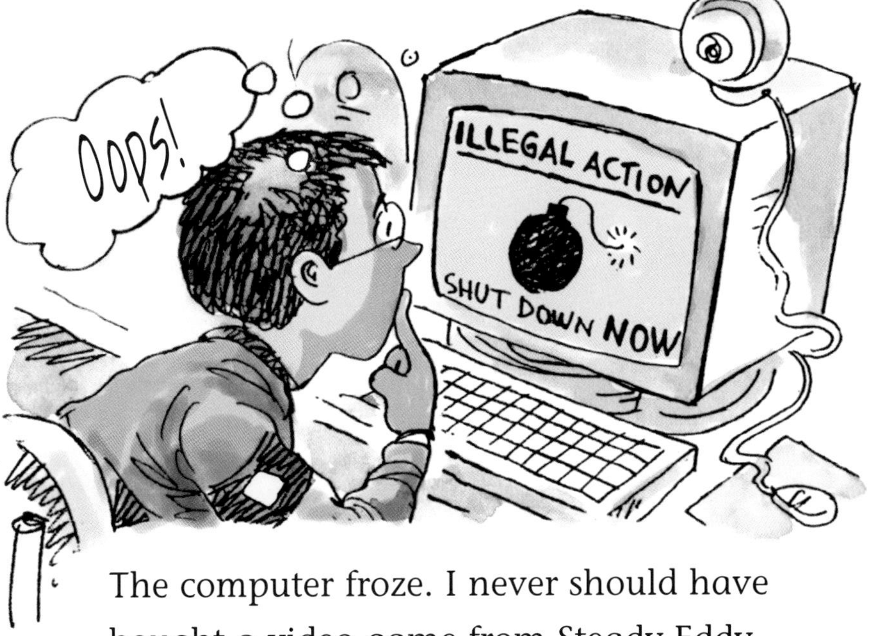
Oops!
ILLEGAL ACTION
SHUT DOWN NOW

The computer froze. I never should have bought a video game from Steady Eddy. Then Dozy walked in. I thought he was going to hit me. But instead, he called a Ridge Riders meeting for the next day, at the round table in the school library.

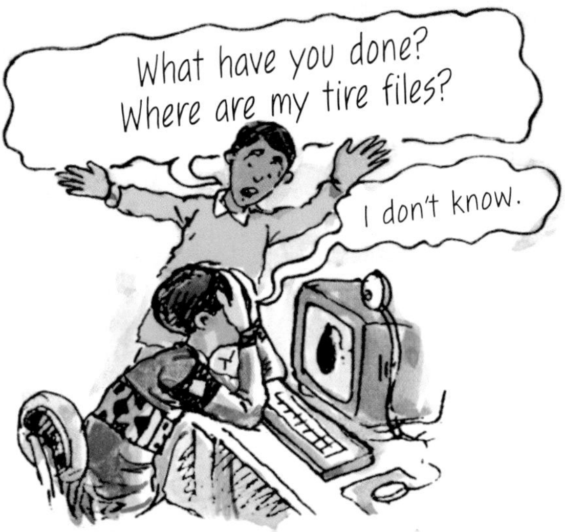
What have you done? Where are my tire files?
I don't know.

The next day:

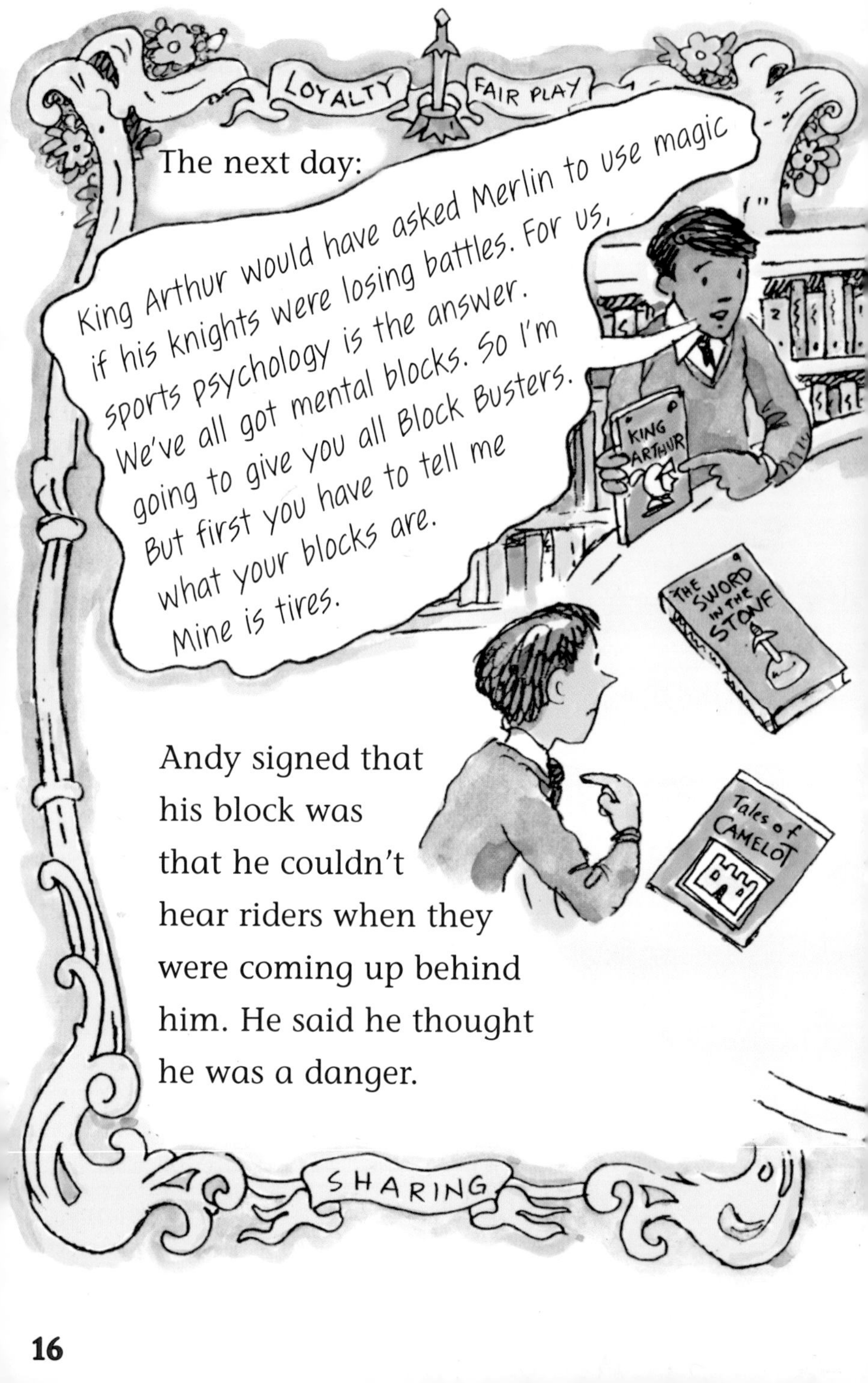
King Arthur would have asked Merlin to use magic if his knights were losing battles. For us, sports psychology is the answer. We've all got mental blocks. So I'm going to give you all Block Busters. But first you have to tell me what your blocks are. Mine is tires.
KING ARTHUR
THE SWORD IN THE STONE
Tales of CAMELOT

Andy signed that his block was that he couldn't hear riders when they were coming up behind him. He said he thought he was a danger.

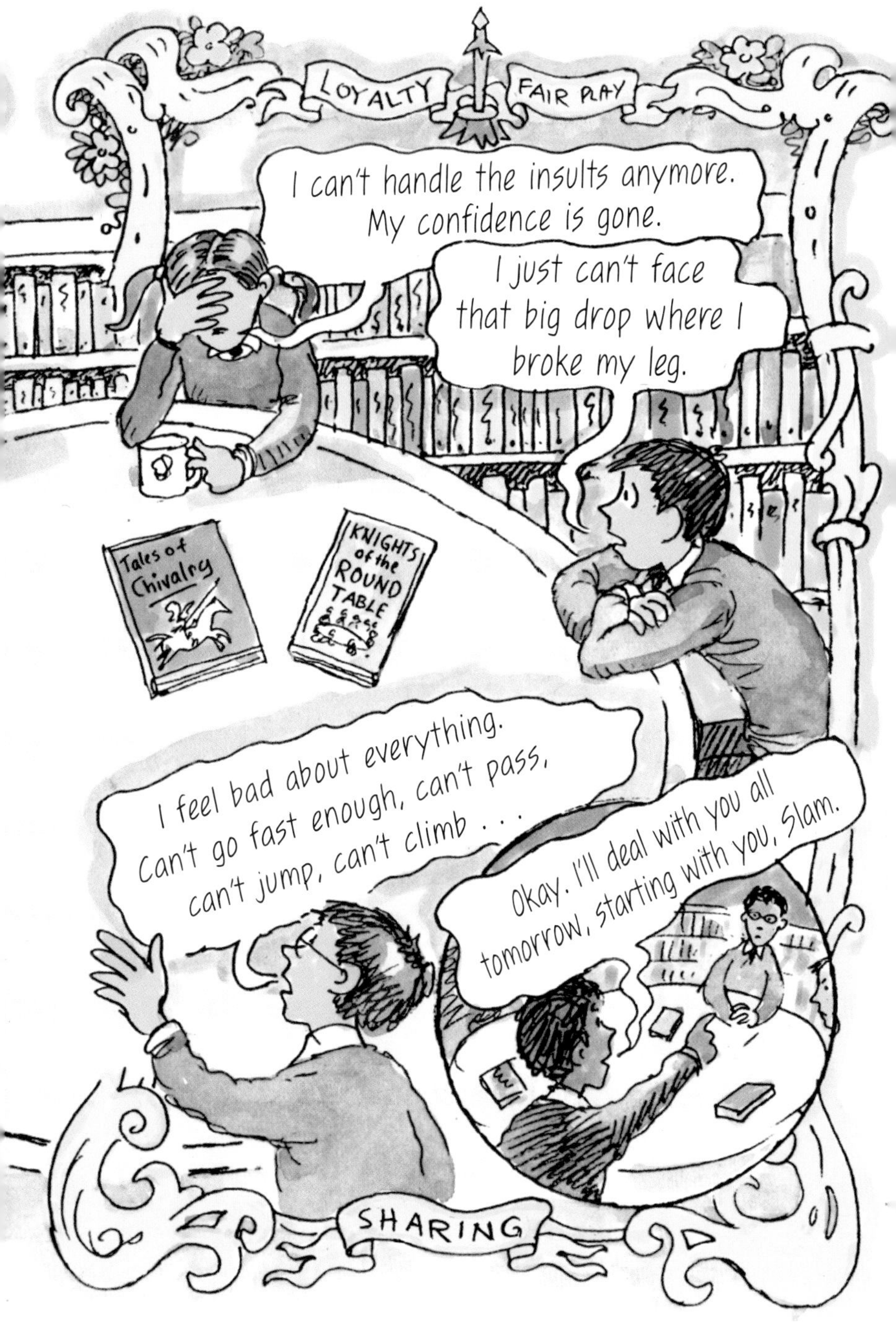
LOYALTY
FAIR PLAY
I can't handle the insults anymore. My confidence is gone.
I just can't face that big drop where I broke my leg.
Tales of Chivalry
KNIGHTS of the ROUND TABLE
I feel bad about everything. Can't go fast enough, can't pass, can't jump, can't climb . . .
Okay. I'll deal with you all tomorrow, starting with you, Slam.
SHARING

The next day . . .

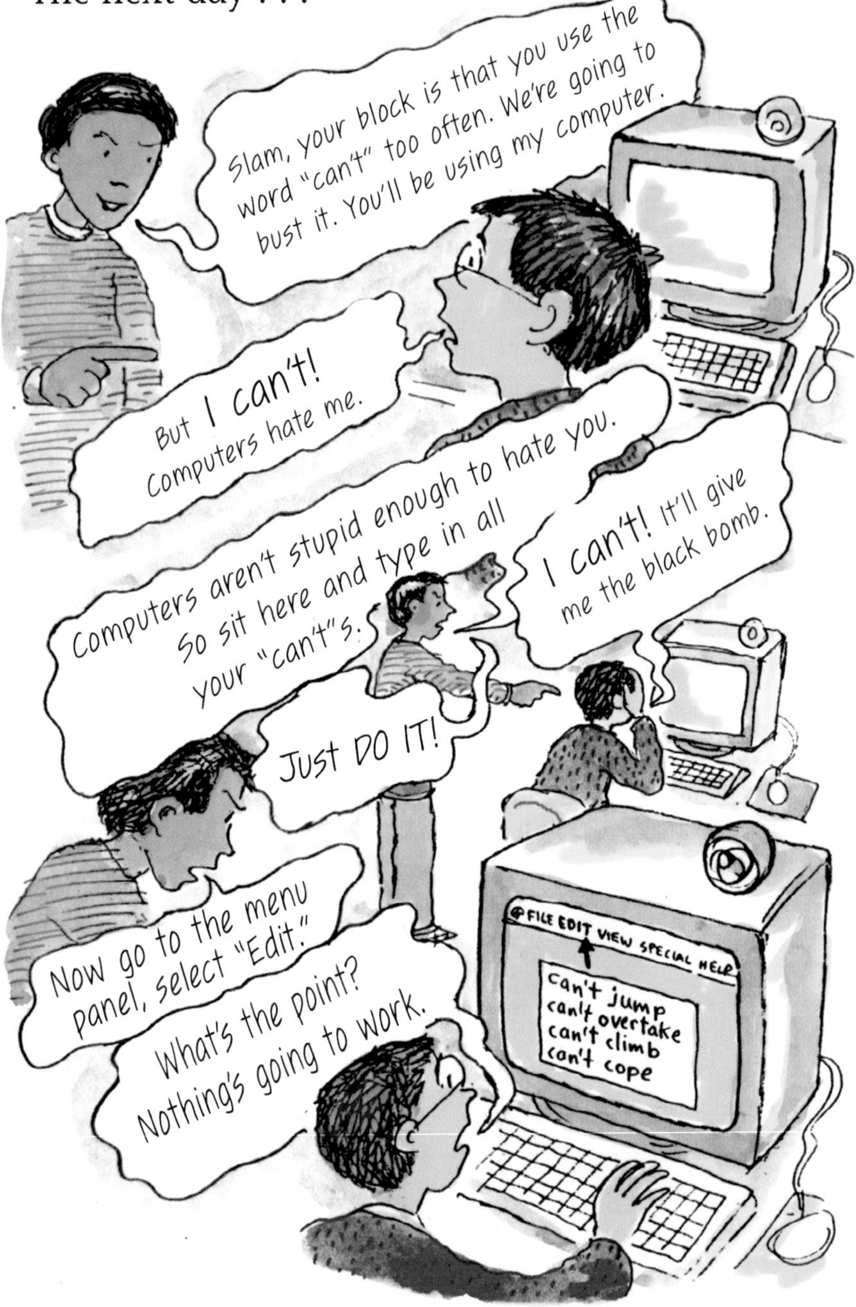

Slam, your block is that you use the word "can't" too often. We're going to bust it. You'll be using my computer.
But I can't! Computers hate me.
Computers aren't stupid enough to hate you. So sit here and type in all your "can't"s.
I can't! It'll give me the black bomb.
JUST DO IT!
Now go to the menu panel, select "Edit."
What's the point? Nothing's going to work.
FILE EDIT VIEW SPECIAL HELP
Can't jump
can't overtake
can't climb
can't cope

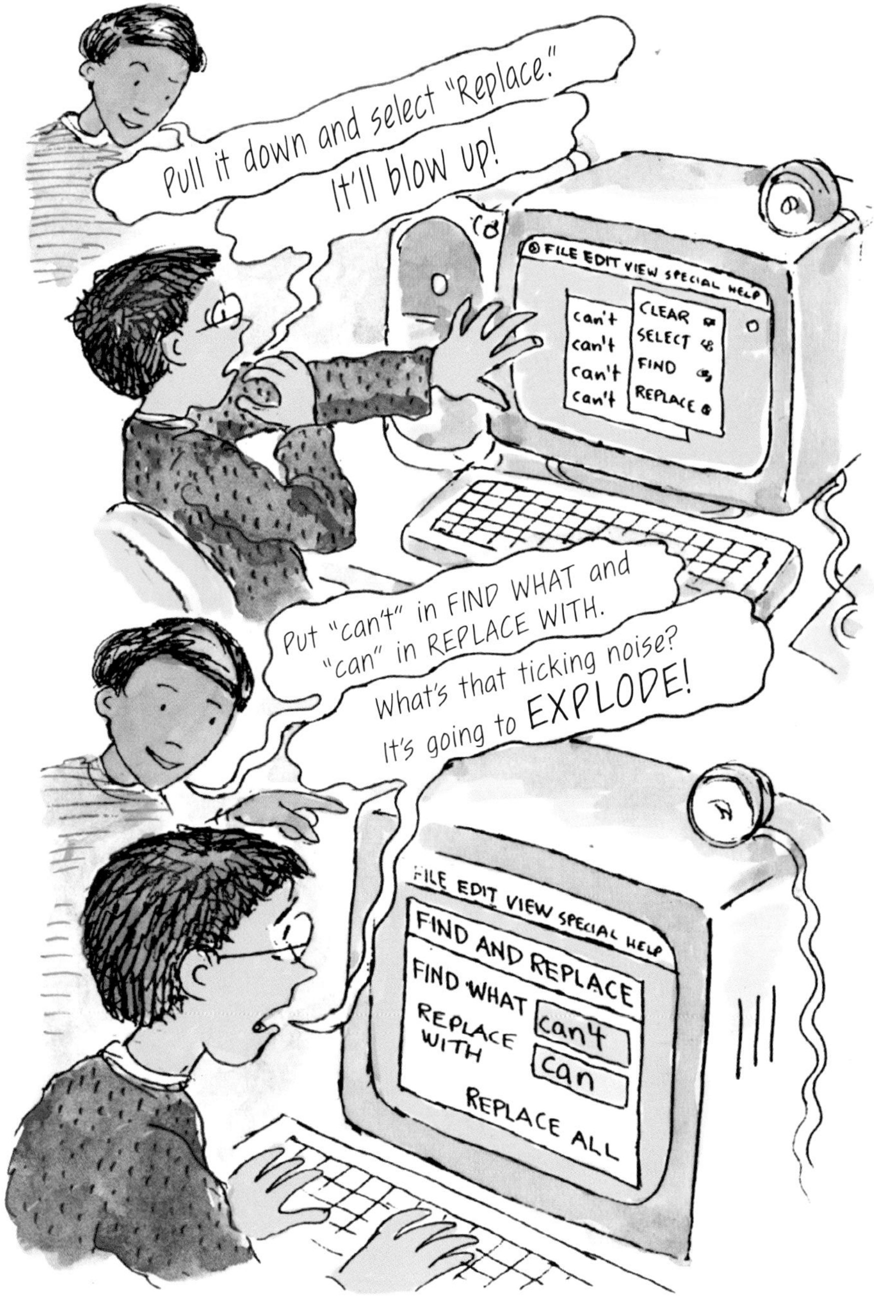

Pull it down and select "Replace."
It'll blow up!
FILE EDIT VIEW SPECIAL HELP
can't
can't
can't
can't
CLEAR
SELECT
FIND
REPLACE
Put "can't" in FIND WHAT and "can" in REPLACE WITH.
What's that ticking noise?
It's going to EXPLODE!
FILE EDIT VIEW SPECIAL HELP
FIND AND REPLACE
FIND WHAT
can't
REPLACE WITH
can
REPLACE ALL

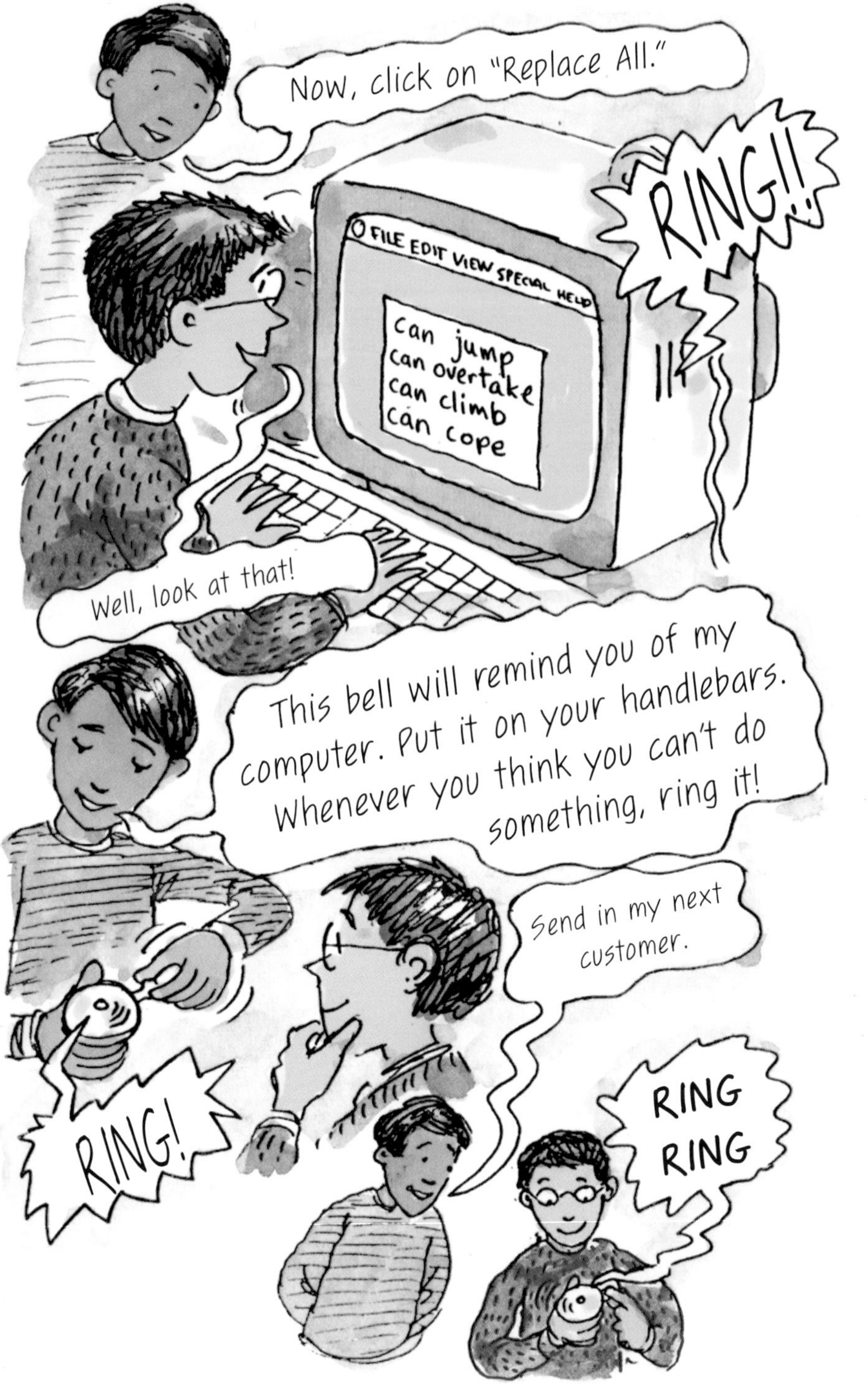
Now, click on "Replace All."
RING!!
FILE EDIT VIEW SPECIAL HELP
can jump
can overtake
can climb
can cope
Well, look at that!
This bell will remind you of my computer. Put it on your handlebars. Whenever you think you can't do something, ring it!
Send in my next customer.
RING!
RING
RING

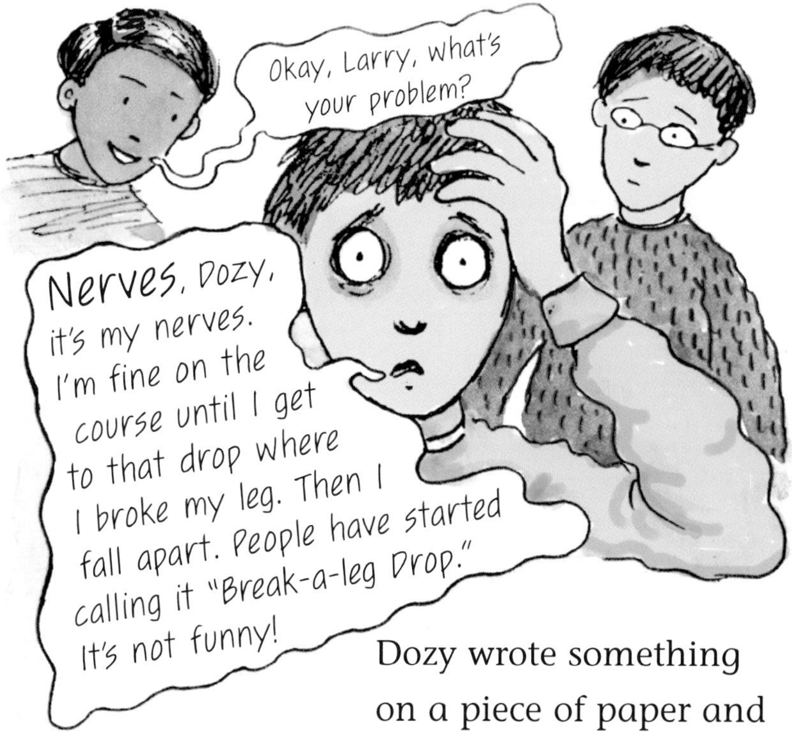
Okay, Larry, what's your problem?
Nerves, Dozy, it's my nerves. I'm fine on the course until I get to that drop where I broke my leg. Then I fall apart. People have started calling it "Break-a-leg Drop." It's not funny!

Dozy wrote something on a piece of paper and put it in an envelope.

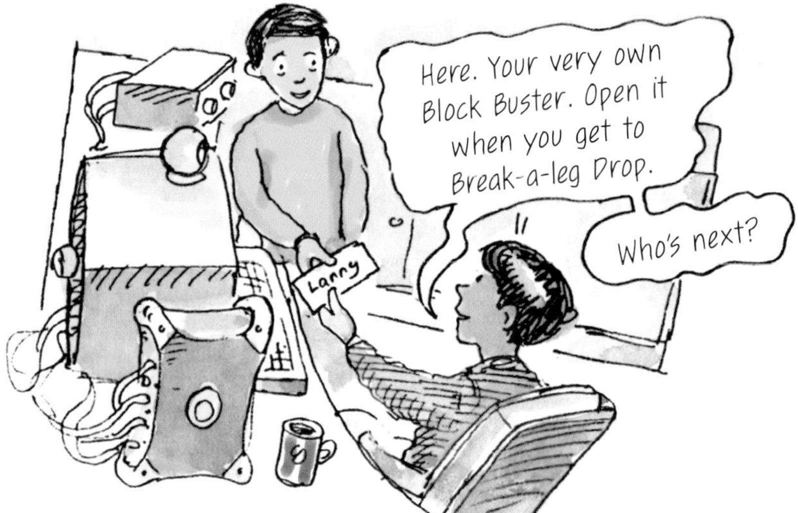
Here. Your very own Block Buster. Open it when you get to Break-a-leg Drop.
Who's next?
Larry

Andy came in. Dozy gave him two rearview mirrors. No one could sneak up on him with those!

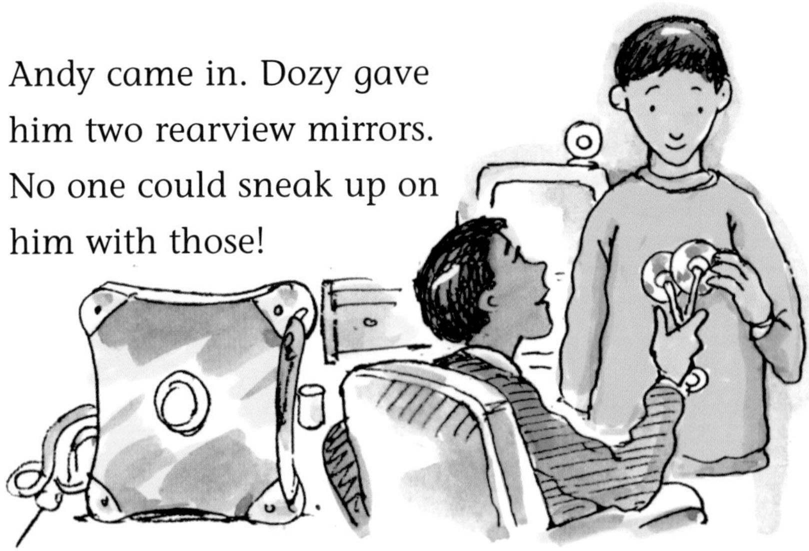

Fiona was next. Dozy knew that Fiona loves shopping. He put her in front of the computer. The screen filled with "Dozy's Victory Shop."

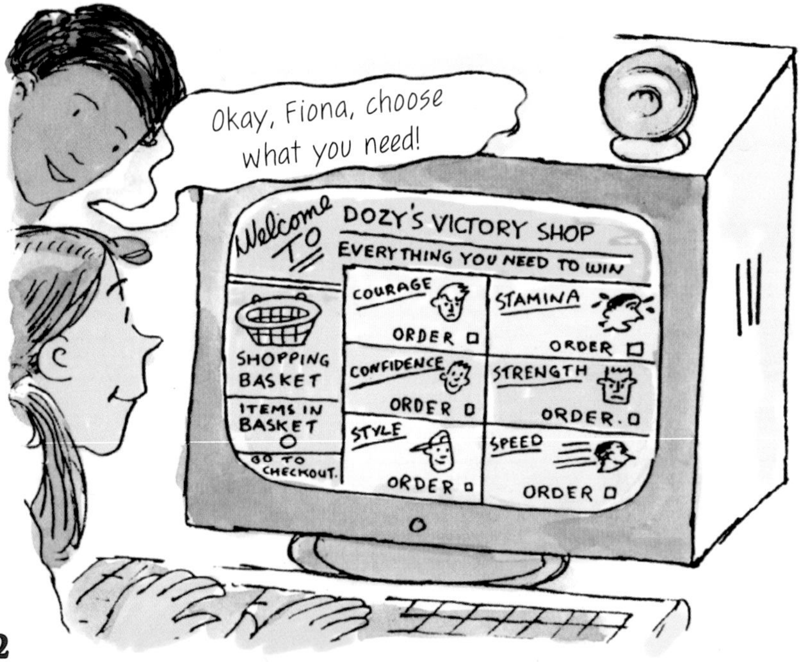
Okay, Fiona, choose what you need!
Welcome TO
DOZY'S VICTORY SHOP
EVERYTHING YOU NEED TO WIN
SHOPPING BASKET
ITEMS IN BASKET
O
GO TO CHECKOUT.
COURAGE
ORDER
STAMINA
ORDER
CONFIDENCE
ORDER
STRENGTH
ORDER.
STYLE
ORDER
SPEED
ORDER

Fiona clicked the order buttons on the items she wanted. Then she clicked "go to checkout."

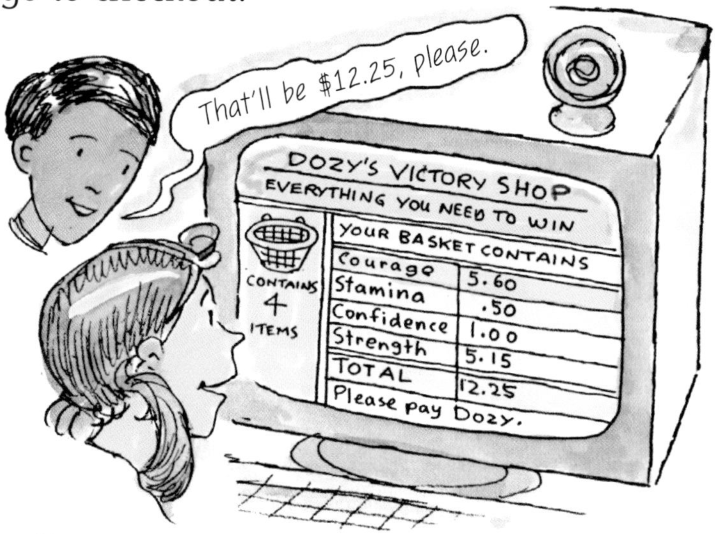
That'll be $12.25, please.
DOZY'S VICTORY SHOP
EVERYTHING YOU NEED TO WIN
YOUR BASKET CONTAINS
Courage 5.60
Stamina .50
Confidence 1.00
Strength 5.15
TOTAL 12.25
Please pay Dozy.
CONTAINS 4 ITEMS

Dozy gave Fiona a little bike basket for her handlebars. It had four packets in it, and a little lid to keep the packets from falling out.

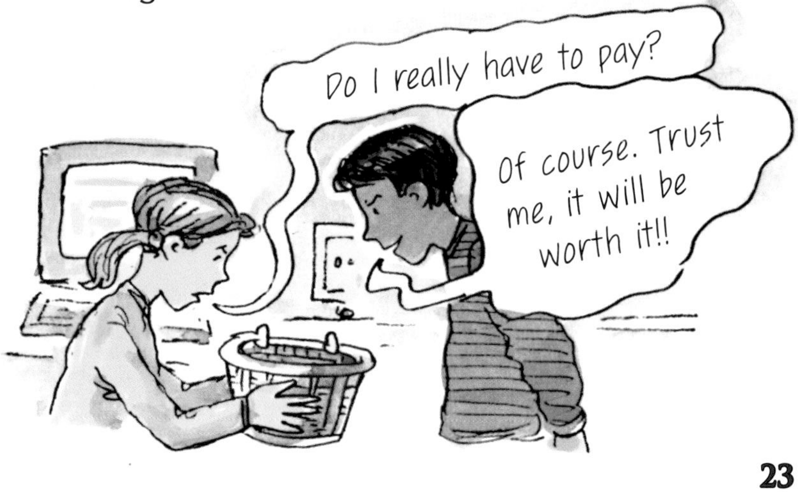
Do I really have to pay?
Of course. Trust me, it will be worth it!!

At 9 a.m. on race day, everyone was at the starting line.

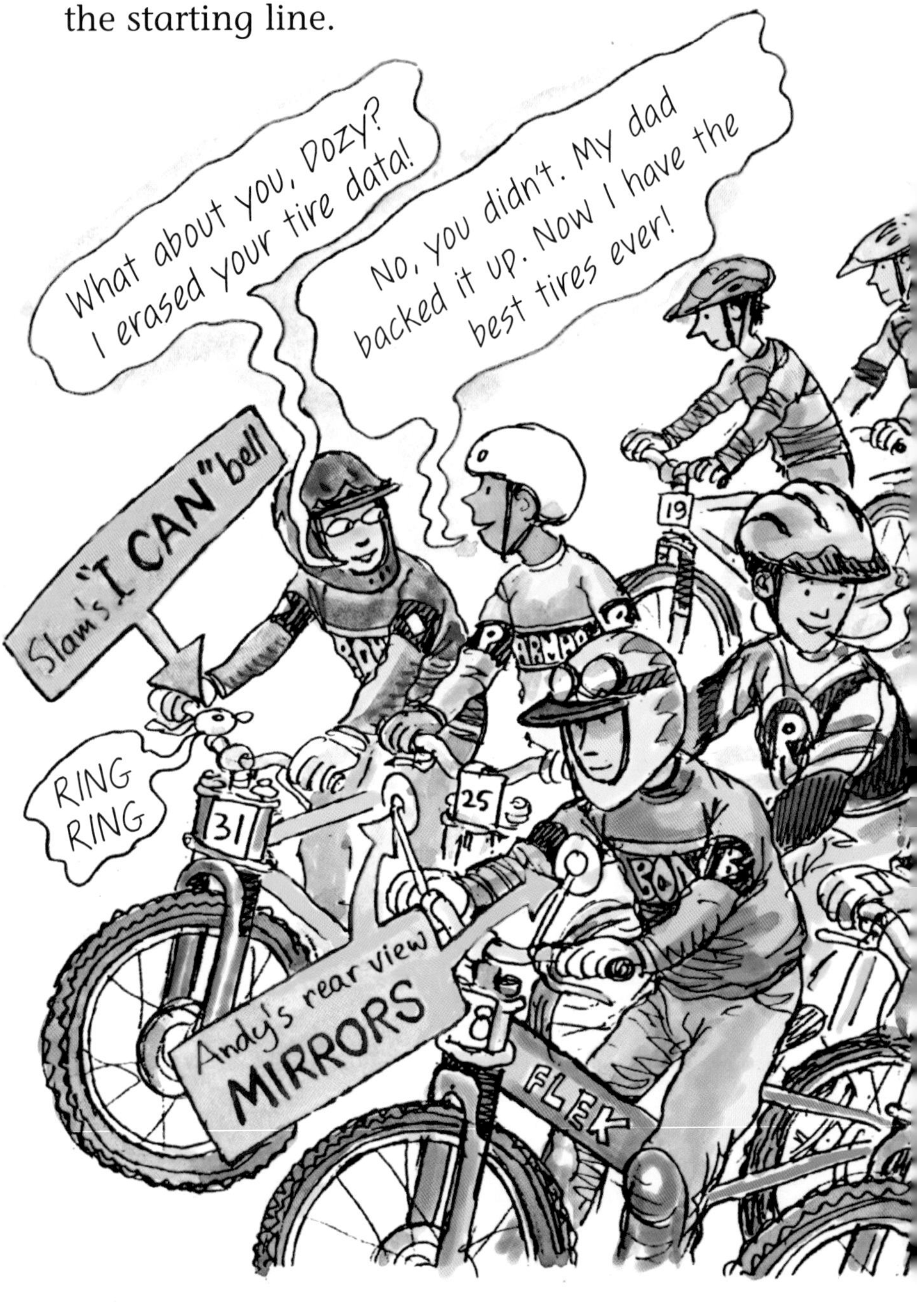
What about you, Dozy? I erased your tire data!
No, you didn't. My dad backed it up. Now I have the best tires ever!
Slam's "I CAN" bell
RING RING
31
25
19
Andy's rear view MIRRORS
FLEK

Boys started first, in the front. Girls lined up in the back. Two six-mile laps were ahead of us.

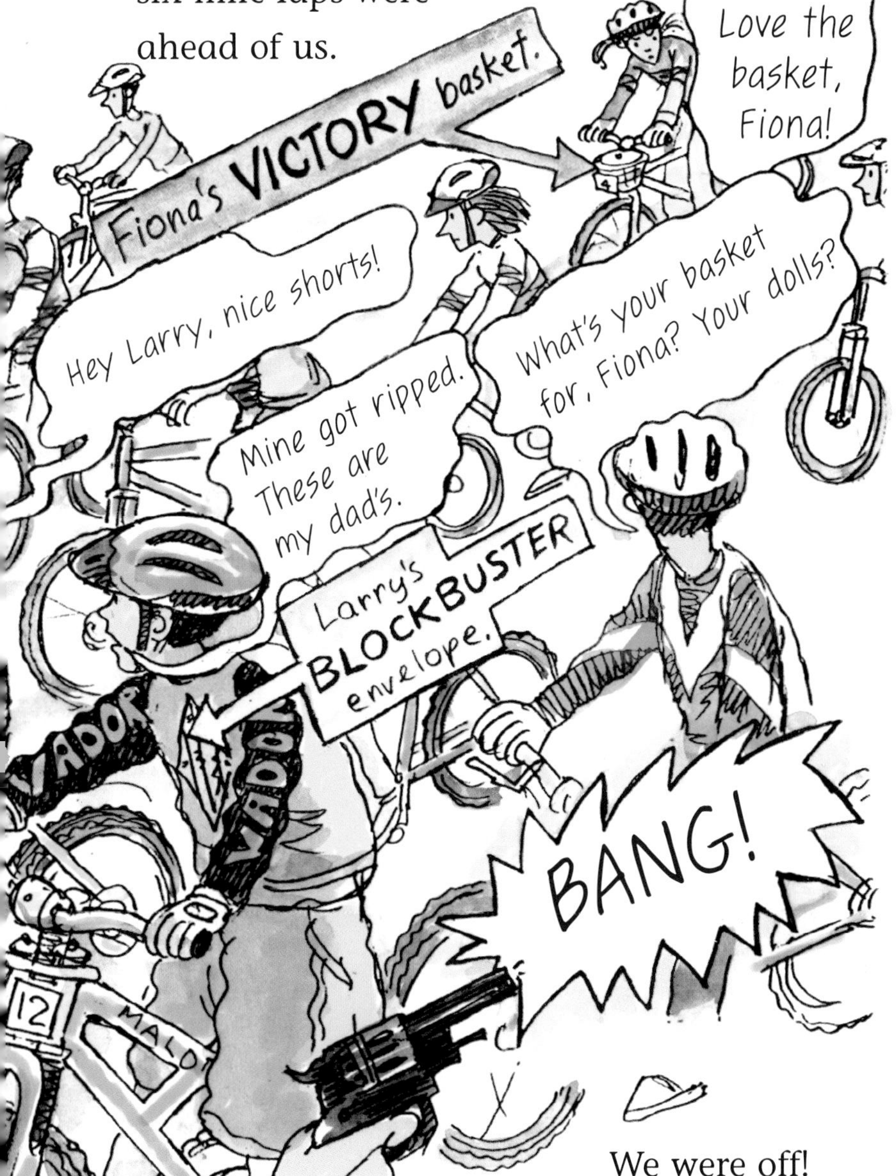
Fiona's VICTORY basket.
WOOOOO! Love the basket, Fiona!
Hey Larry, nice shorts!
Mine got ripped. These are my dad's.
What's your basket for, Fiona? Your dolls?
Larry's BLOCKBUSTER envelope.
12
MALO
BANG!

We were off!

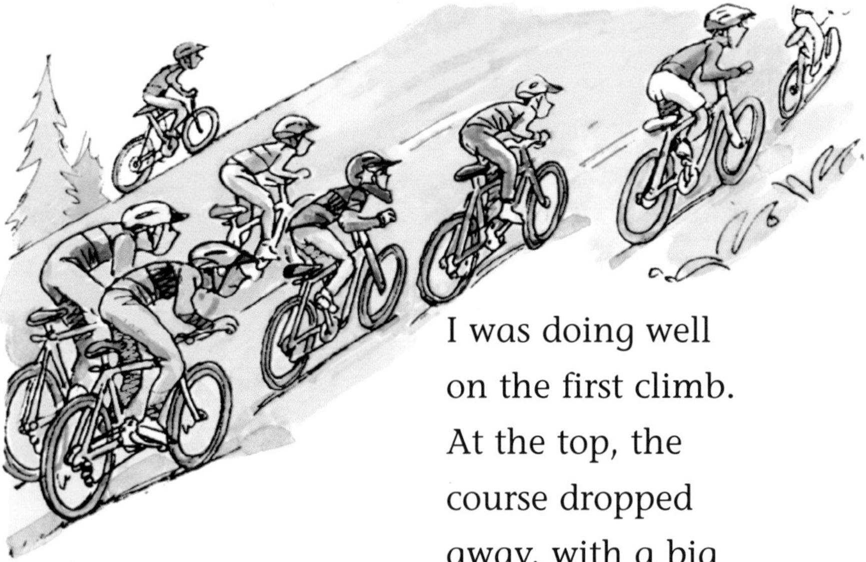

I was doing well
on the first climb.
At the top, the
course dropped
away, with a big
jump at the bottom.

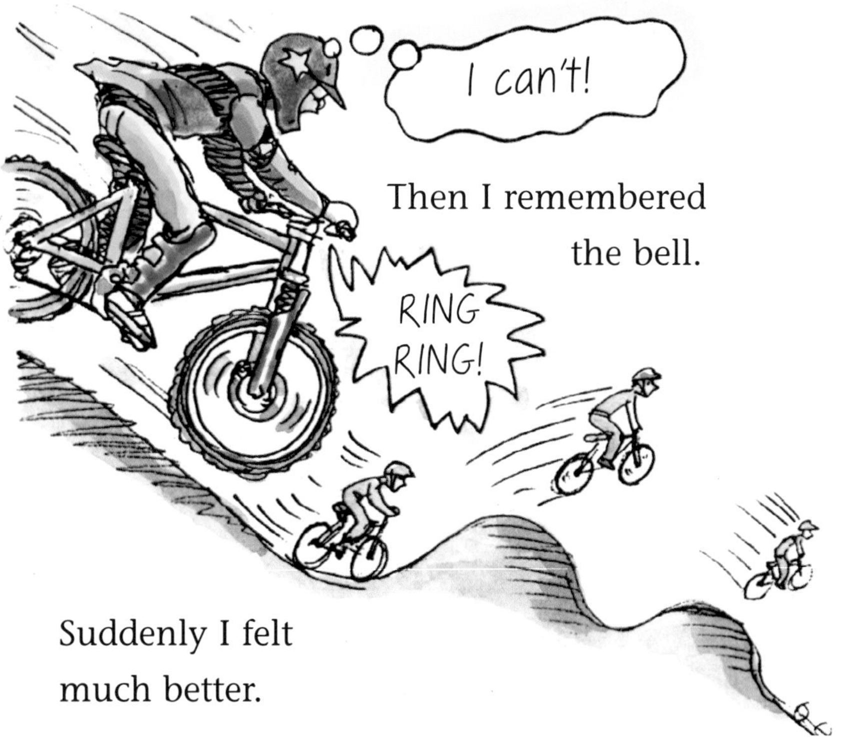
I can't!
RING RING!

Then I remembered
the bell.

Suddenly I felt
much better.

RING RING!

It was like magic. Dozy's "Replace" idea had worked.

OOOOOOOOOOOOHHHHHHHHHHHH!!!!

It was one of my best jumps ever.

Five minutes later, I looked behind me. Fiona was right there.

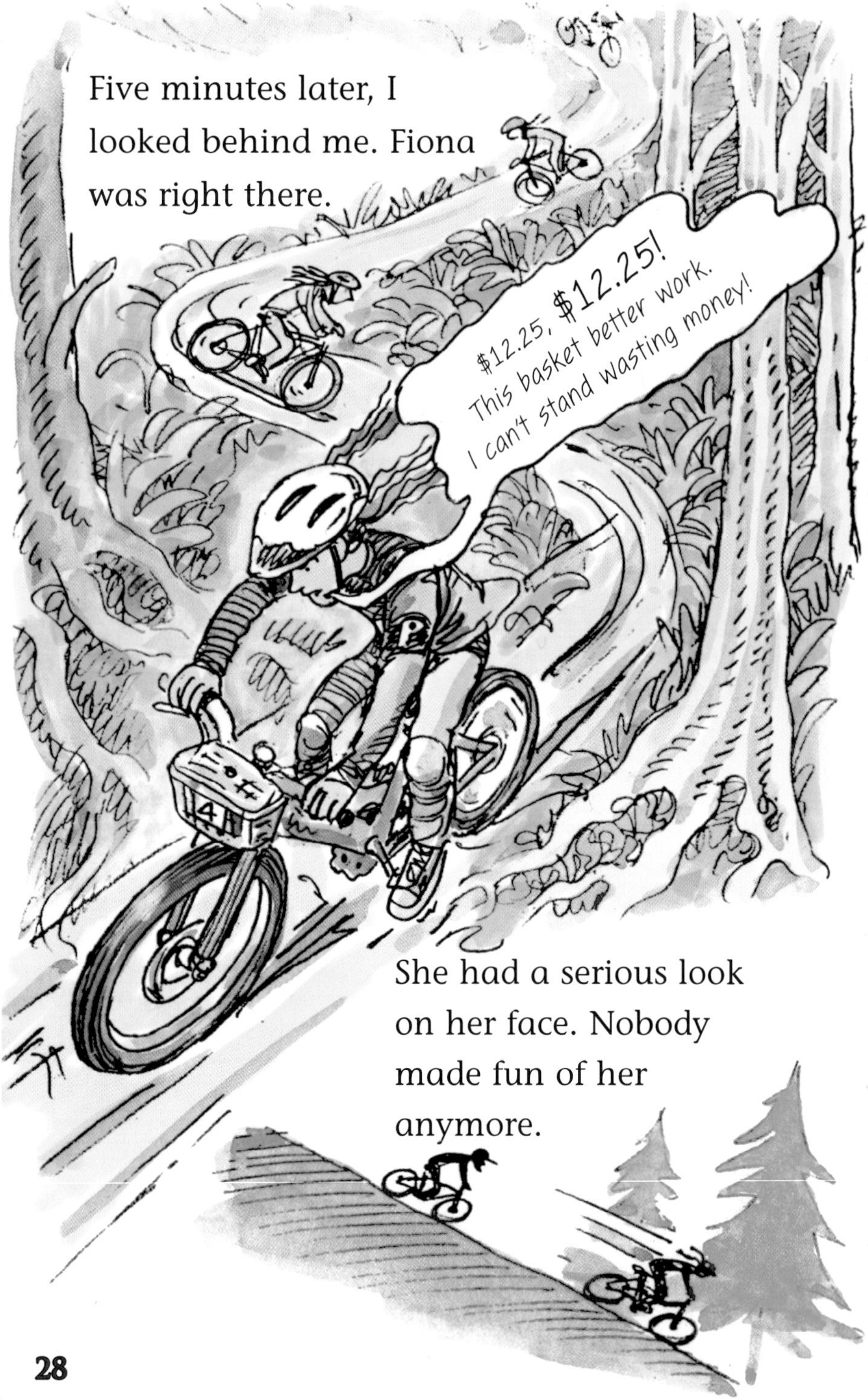

$12.25, $12.25!
This basket better work.
I can't stand wasting money!
14

She had a serious look on her face. Nobody made fun of her anymore.

Then I came up behind Larry. He had stopped at the edge of Break-a-leg Drop.

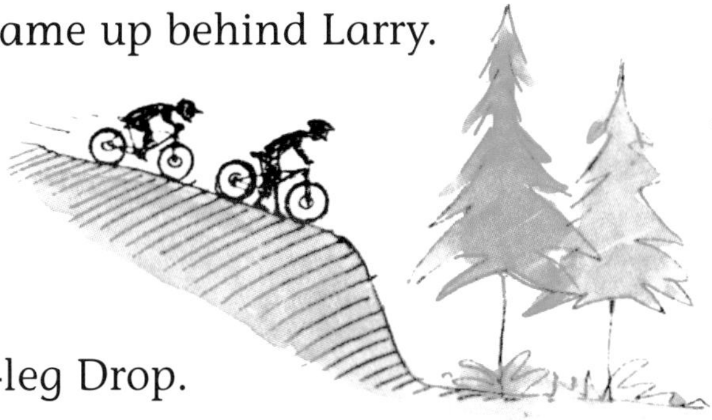

I saw him open his Block Buster envelope and start laughing.

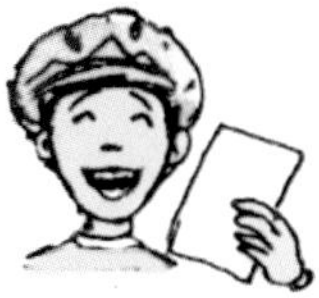

Still laughing, he pulled up his baggy shorts, stood on the pedals, got his weight over the back wheel, and rode down the drop like a pro.

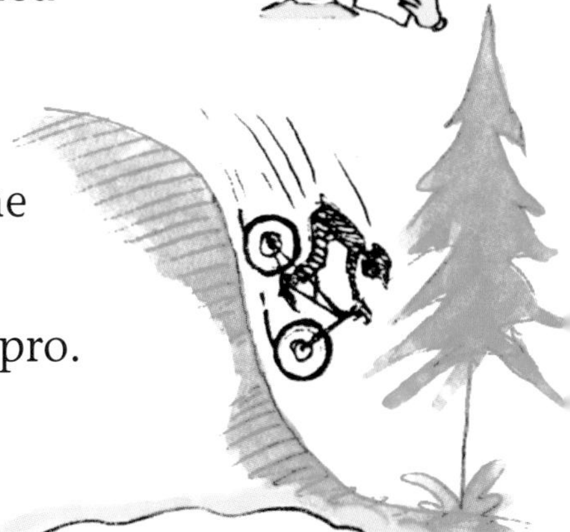

I followed him down.

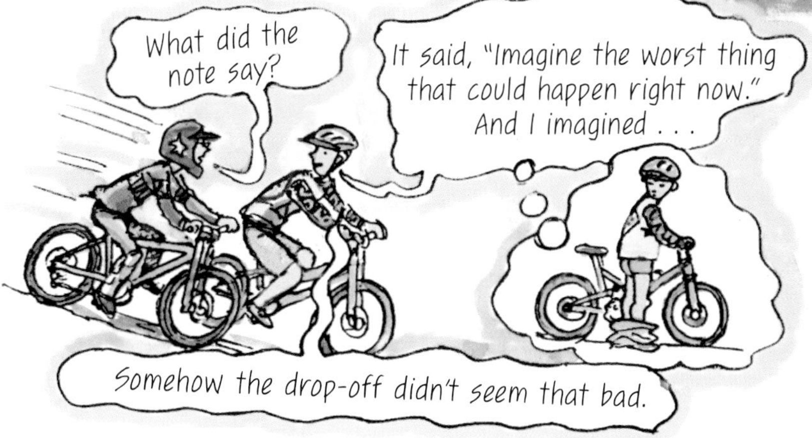
What did the note say?
It said, "Imagine the worst thing that could happen right now." And I imagined . . .
Somehow the drop-off didn't seem that bad.

At the bottom of the last climb, we saw Dozy grinding his way up through the mud. His carefully chosen tires were really working well for him. He was just behind Andy, who was trying to catch the main pack of riders.

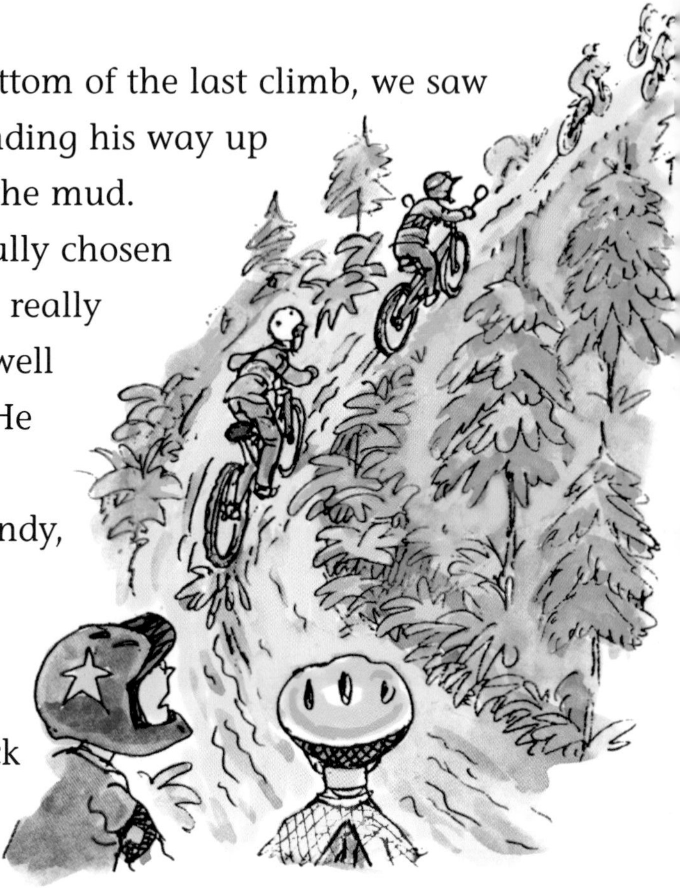

We went up after them, but there was no way we were ever going to catch them.

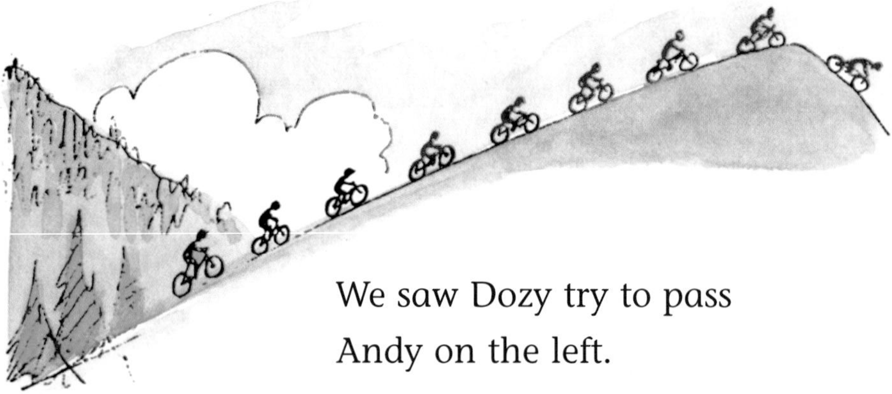

We saw Dozy try to pass Andy on the left.

Andy saw him in his mirror and blocked him.

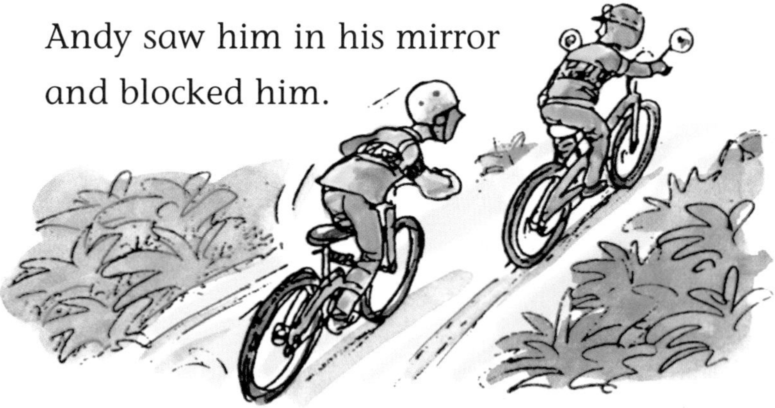

Then Dozy tried to pass on the right. Andy saw that, too, and put on a burst of speed, leaving Dozy way behind.

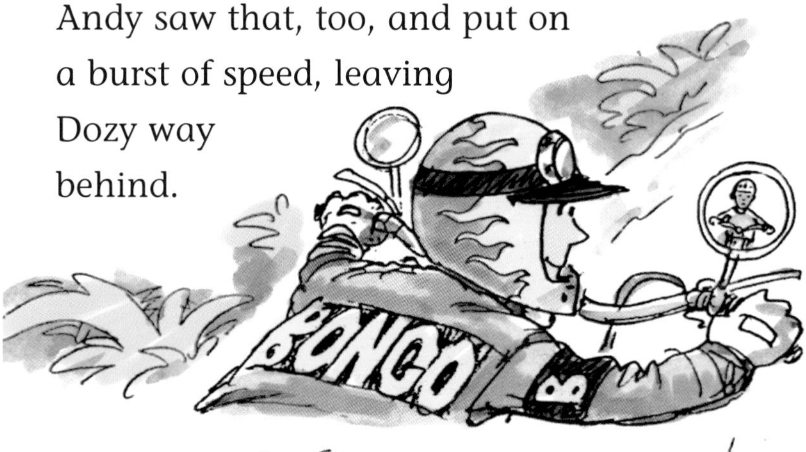
BONGO
B

We got to the top just in time to see Andy roaring past the pack on the last hill before the finish line.

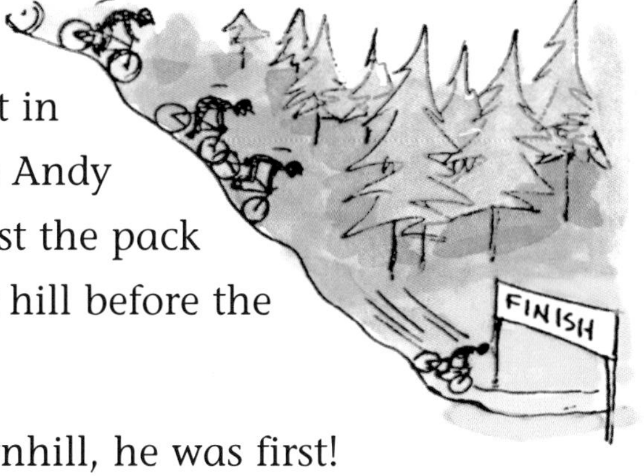
FINISH

Going downhill, he was first!

It was close, but Andy came in first and Fiona, not far behind, won the girls' race.

While they were getting their prizes, Larry and I thanked Dozy for his help.

We had all scored some points for the Sword in the Stump Challenge.

Later that night, Dozy and I were checking his e-mail. There was one from Andy:

Mirror mirror, left and right,
Keeping Dozy in my sight.
Thanks to him I won the race,
But as a friend, he's in first place.

Andy

About the Author and Illustrator

Robin and Chris Lawrie wrote the *Ridge Riders* books together, and Robin illustrated them. Their inspiration for these books is their son. They wanted to write books that he would find interesting. Many of the *Ridge Riders* books are based on adventures he and his friends had while biking.

Robin and Chris live in England, and will soon be moving to a big, old house that is also home to sixty bats.

Glossary

block (BLOK)—something that stops someone

challenge (CHAL-uhnj)—something difficult that requires extra work or effort to do

confidence (KON-fuh-duhnss)—belief in your own abilities

determined (di-TUR-mind)—if you're determined to do something, you made a decision to do it

install (in-STAWL)—to put something into place, ready to be used

psychology (sye-KOH-luh-jee)—the study of the mind, emotions, and human behavior

reactions (ree-AK-shuhnz)—actions in response to something else

series (SEER-eez)—a group of related things that follow in order

spectators (SPEK-tay-turz)—people who are watching an event

sportsmanship (SPORTS-muhn-ship)—fair and respectful behavior

victory (VIK-tuh-ree)—a win in a contest

Internet Sites

Do you want to know more about subjects related to this book? Or are you interested in learning about other topics? Then check out FactHound, a fun, easy way to find Internet sites.

Our investigative staff has already sniffed out great sites for you!

Here's how to use FactHound:

1. Visit *www.facthound.com*

2. Select your grade level.

3. To learn more about subjects related to this book, type in the book's ISBN number: **9781434204844**.

4. Click the **Fetch It** button.

FactHound will fetch the best Internet sites for you!

Discussion Questions

1. Why did the Block Busters that Dozy invented work? How did the Block Busters help the Ridge Riders get over their fears?

2. Why does Andy send Dozy an e-mail at the end of this book? What does the e-mail mean?

3. On page 16, Dozy talks about King Arthur. Do you know any King Arthur stories? Who are the Knights of the Round Table?

Writing Prompts

1. Do you have any blocks that stop you from doing things? Imagine that Dozy is inventing a Block Buster for you. What would it be?

2. The Ridge Riders ride their bikes together, but they're also good friends. Do you play any sports or do any organized activities with your friends? Does it help your friendship? Has it ever hurt your friendship? Write about it.

3. What are some other ways that the Ridge Riders could have gotten over their problems? Pick one of the Ridge Riders, and make a plan that person could use to get past his or her block.

More downhill fun . . .

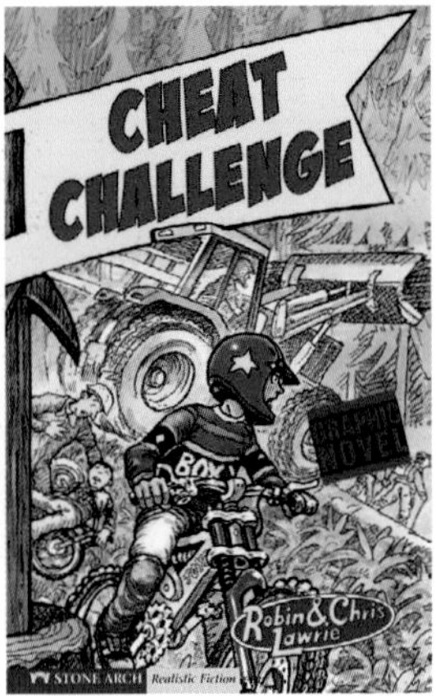
CHEAT CHALLENGE
GRAPHIC NOVEL
Robin & Chris Lawrie
STONE ARCH Realistic Fiction

Cheat Challenge

Slam Duncan accidentally gets a look at the map of a new racing course. He knows he can't tell his teammates the course's secrets. But when practicing puts his friends in danger, what is he supposed to do?

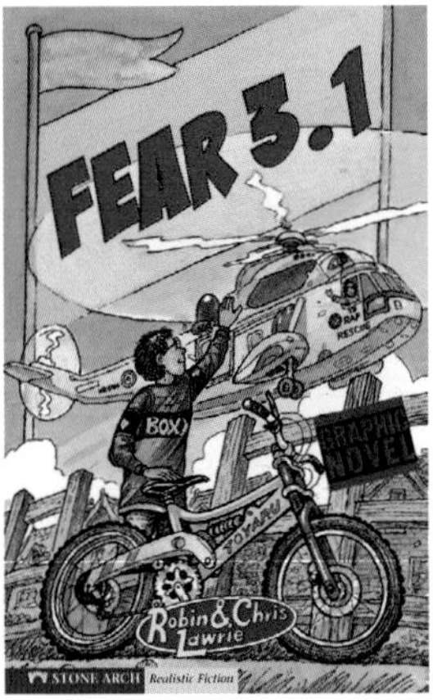
FEAR 3.1
GRAPHIC NOVEL
Robin & Chris Lawrie
STONE ARCH Realistic Fiction

Fear 3.1

Rock climbing used to be one of Slam Duncan's favorite things to do for fun. But one day, Slam loses his foothold. He doesn't get hurt, but that doesn't stop Slam from being terrified. Can Slam ever get over this phobia for good?

. . . with the Ridge Riders!

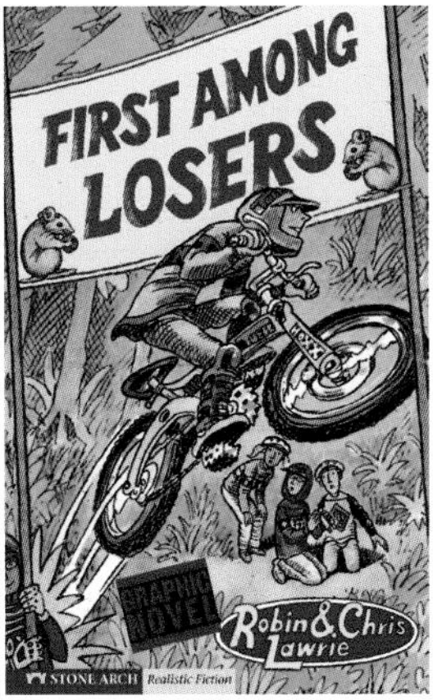
FIRST AMONG LOSERS
GRAPHIC NOVEL
Robin & Chris Lawrie
STONE ARCH
Realistic Fiction

First Among Losers

Slam Duncan is determined to beat his arch rival, Punk Tuer. Unfortunately, Punk doesn't fight fair. Punk thinks he can buy victory, until he realizes he may actually need the Ridge Riders' help. They have to teach Punk a lesson about what it means to race together like a team.

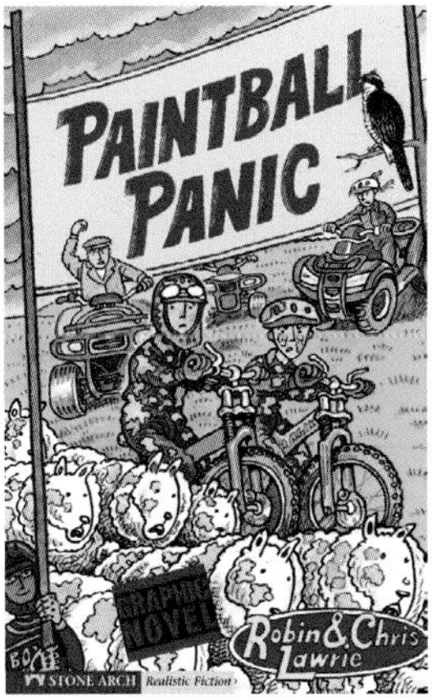
PAINTBALL PANIC
GRAPHIC NOVEL
Robin & Chris Lawrie
STONE ARCH
Realistic Fiction

Paintball Panic

The Ridge Riders won't let property developers take over Westridge, the hill where they train. So when the developers try to have a paintball weekend on the hill, their fun quickly backfires. The Ridge Riders want to save Westridge—hopefully, their neighbors do too!

Check out more Stone Arch Books sports books!

JAKE MADDOX
BMX
Bully
STONE ARCH Realistic Fiction

BMX Bully
by Jake Maddox

Matt's chances of making the Evergreen Racing Team are seriously threatened when Tyler moves into town. If Tyler would stop cheating, Matt might actually have a chance of making the team.

JAKE MADDOX
MOTOCROSS
DOUBLE-CROSS
STONE ARCH Realistic Fiction

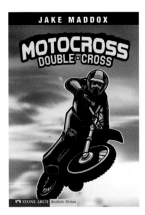

Motocross Double-cross
by Jake Maddox

A race to determine who goes to the Nationals is separating Carlos and Ricky, and someone seems to be sabotaging their bikes. Has the competition made them turn against each other? Can they figure out who's pulling a double-cross?